NOISY NEIGHBORS

Ruth Green

NOiSY NEIGHBORS

Ruth Green

Sid the snail wants a nap in his favorite tree.

But those **chirping** sparrows are as **loud** as can be!

The veggie patch
is cozy and
quite quiet too.

Till the **singing** foxes
make a **hullabaloo.**

But the bees
buzz so **loudly,**
it just isn't fair!

The ducks are **quacking** and **splashing** around.

The owls are hooting
in the dark of the wood.

And the badgers
are **chattering,**
it's really no good.

But tired little Sid
soon has an idea,
to stop all this **racket**,
the answer is clear.

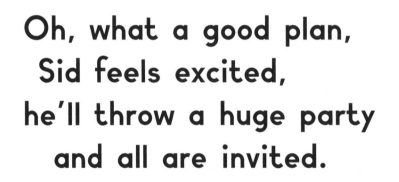

Oh, what a good plan,
Sid feels excited,
he'll throw a huge party
and all are invited.

And **WOW!**
What a **blast!**
They have
such a **ball!**

And get so tired out,
they fall asleep,
one and all.

First published 2011 by order of the Tate Trustees
by Tate Publishing, a division of Tate Enterprises Ltd,
Millbank, London SW1P 4RG
www.tate.org.uk/publishing

A catalogue record for this book
is available from the British Library
ISBN: 978 1 85437 942 9 (UK edition)

Distributed in the United States and Canada by
Harry N. Abrams, Inc., New York
ISBN: 978 1 85437 994 8 (North American edition)
Library of Congress control number: 2010940866

Designed by Godfrey Design
Colour reproduction by Evergreen Colour
Separation Co. Ltd, Hong Kong
Printed and bound in China by
C&C Offset Printing Co., Ltd